Tessa-Kate Curtis grew up in Hertfordshire, but now lives in Cambridgeshire with her husband Stuart, where she works full-time as a medical secretary. They live with their two dogs, Zeke and Nova, plus two large cats, Rocco and Tino – who think they are dogs. Tessa-Kate loves her weekends with Stu, particularly walking the dogs in woodlands or coastline, and exploring new trails. She enjoys swimming and cycling (occasionally), plus watching movies at the cinema – or at home. She is also really happy when burying her nose in an exceptionally good crime thriller novel.

FAIRIES at Number 55

TESSA-KATE CURTIS

AUSTIN MACAULEY PUBLISHERS™
LONDON • CAMBRIDGE • NEW YORK • SHARJAH

A CIP catalogue record for this title is available from the British Library.

ISBN 9781398470453 (Paperback)
ISBN 9781398470460 (ePub e-book)

www.austinmacauley.com

First Published 2022
Austin Macauley Publishers Ltd®
1 Canada Square
Canary Wharf
London
E14 5AA

To my mum, Shirley, for reading to me as a small child,
nurturing my imagination and instilling my love of reading
and writing always;
To Mrs Powell, my first teacher for encouraging my stories
even at five years of age;
To Stuart, my husband and love, for believing in me;
To darling Skeet, the most handsome and gentlest dog,
gone but adored forever.

Austin Macauley, of course, for believing in my fairies and
giving them the chance to be seen and heard.

Fairies at Number 55

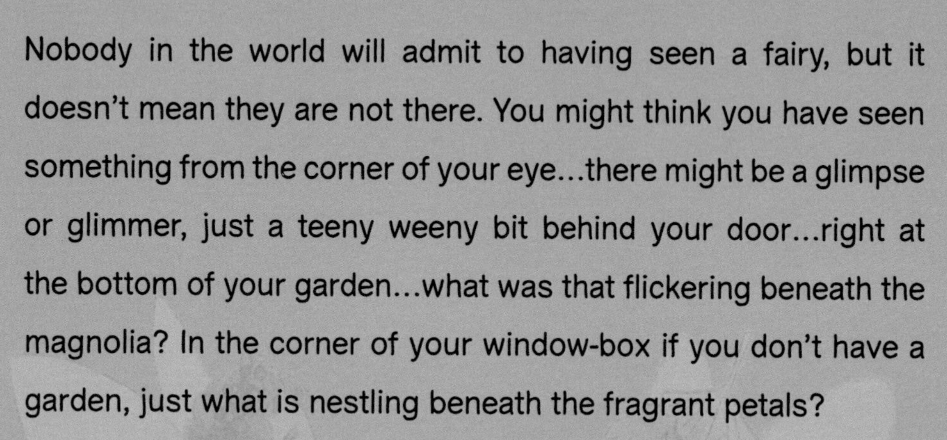

Nobody in the world will admit to having seen a fairy, but it doesn't mean they are not there. You might think you have seen something from the corner of your eye...there might be a glimpse or glimmer, just a teeny weeny bit behind your door...right at the bottom of your garden...what was that flickering beneath the magnolia? In the corner of your window-box if you don't have a garden, just what is nestling beneath the fragrant petals?

For hundreds and hundreds of years, all over the world, toys in a toy box have been rearranged, pens and pencils in a pencil box changed to a colour sequence to match a rainbow...your favourite dolls or action figures moved from where you left them when you played last. Now they have a new action scene, or your baby doll has been snuggled into a cosy blanket that you don't remember placing around her chubby arms. Fairies are kind and they always, always do the sweetest, gentlest things for you and for all that you love, but rarely will they be visible. But, you just never know...

I know there are fairies at number 55 because I have been privileged to see them... I know also that they have names: Mimosa is the sunny, bright and cheerful older 'sister' to her family. Always in bright yellow, it's amazing she is not spotted whenever she is out and about in that garden. I suppose you see her and think it is a sun spot just there at the edge of the patio.

Chicory, on the other hand, is always in violet or blue shades... she is more inclined to be spotted (if she might be) on branches of trees or the log pile at the foot of the garden; she embraces the woody, shadier places and makes friends with woodland creatures such as Hettie the Hedgehog or Bertie Badger. Her twin Chirrup is a noisy, chattering brother. He mimics the birds with whom he shares a branch. The birds know him so well and chatter to him and ask which gardens are putting out most feed for them, to save their wing activity and take the shortest journeys to a full tummy. Chirrup tries to sing with the song thrush and it is a delight to hear his efforts. You won't know it is a fairy chirruping; you will think, from your bedroom window, it is a baby fledgling learning to sing!

Lychen and Moss are sturdy, hardworking boy fairies. They will keep clear entry access for Hettie Hedgehog to get in and out of your garden. If that pile of twigs, or your dog's toys, seem to block that little gap beneath your fence, either of the two, dark-green-clad fairies will drop down from their cosy nook and expertly move the frisbee, or your football, and ensure that Hettie can get through as she needs to under cover of darkness.

The only other fairy I have seen at number 55 is the fairy family's mum, Starlight. Sheer gossamer wings with a duck-egg blue hue. She is beautiful, her tinkling voice always sounds like tiny cymbals chinking as she laughs, forever checking her fairy family, imploring them not to be naughty, but to keep kindness and gentleness to the fore of every endeavour.

In which Hettie Needs a Hand and Hitches a Ride

Hettie is the sweetest, gentlest of hedgehogs. Flashing, beady eyes blink from beneath the prickly surround but they are looking for her next breakfast. Out in the earliest of hours, she snuffles and hoinks between garden gates and fences. Hoping that kindly "giants" will have placed a saucer of their kitty's food where she might easily trundle along and come upon it, to savour the moist morsels. Yesterday, though, Hettie inadvertently trod upon the sharpest of thorns and her little tootsies are sore and tender. She is not making such good progress and it is taking forever to do her regular route. She is, indeed, snuffling, but is sore too and feeling the teeniest bit grumpy.

Lychen and Moss have seen Hettie slowly and deliberately making her way. They know she is hungry and needs to feed. They have been playing in a 'giant family's' garden and know just how to help! They clap their hands, shake out their gossamer wings – in a muddy, dark green shade – and rise and rise... Tucked in the giant family's garden is a young giant's toy. Lychen thinks he overheard it is called a cakebald...in any event, it is a platform that has small circular objects that revolve at speed as the smallest giant stands and pedals on the platform. Lychen zooms in to the corner of the garden where this 'toy' has been discarded. The smaller giant now has bigger circular things to

rotate and move on. Lychen thinks this must be a 'tyke'. Either way, the cakebald (which we readers know is a skateboard) is free and available for Hettie to climb on to and make her way much more effectively to the next garden where the household kitty has, indeed, shared her grub. Flying at speed on this toy, Lychen and Moss push and push forward, mustering all their fairy strength before they brake hard at Hettie and, in unison, delight in telling her it is available for her to climb on and glide onwards. Using the tootsies that are not sore, Hettie thanks those cheerful fairies for their great help and does, indeed, climb aboard and glide onward to her breakfast. Lychen and Moss clap their hands together now at another good job done!

Red Tod Finds Love and Is No Longer Lonely

Behind ‘No. 55’, there runs a leafy, green bridleway. Cool and peaceful, gossamer cobwebs and ‘cuckoo spit’ hover over the varying shades of green...nettles, grasses, dandelions and daisies. The bridleway runs around the perimeter of the village and there are numerous birds’ nests as well as numerous insect homes in and around the logs and ground-spreading ivies and undergrowth. Secretly, within a particular shaded and cool spot lives ‘Red Tod’. A handsome and noble dog-fox. He lives alone and lopes along the bridleway in the early hours before breakfast, or in the dusky shades of tea time. He plucks berries from the bushes and thinks, much as he loves his solitary existence, he would really, really love to have a companion and perhaps cubs to share his jaunts with.

Chicory and Chirrup watch him frequently and admire his russet red, gleaming and glossy coat. They watch him nimbly plucking fruits and managing to never prick his nose on the gorse bushes. They call to him from time to time, and he looks up to their branches and nods, in a gentlemanly fashion, at them. Indeed, if he wore a cap, he would politely doff it at them.

As he passed early one morning, Chicory turned to Chirrup and declared, “Red Tod is lonely! He is so handsome and noble, there MUST be a companion for him somewhere nearby.”

Chirrup nodded, deep in thought, then gasped. "Yes, YES, there must be a friend for him... I know just the vixen. You know, at the other end of the village, there is Vixie...that cheeky, playful puppy-like vixen! She told me a long time ago that her wise mummy vixen told her and her cub siblings that the time had come to venture out into the great wide world and make their own families."

Chicory clapped her hands and declared, "We can't hang about here, we must make them meet, but how?"

The twin fairies shook out their wings and rose to the cool skies to seek out Mimosa. She would know exactly how to make this happen.

It wasn't hard to spot Mimosa...gleaming and glinting bright yellow, she was atop a garden fence, admiring a row of beautiful nodding sunflowers in exactly the same shade of yellow.

"Mimosa, Mimosa...you must help us," the twins chattered in unison.

Mimosa replied with a chuckle, "Just how can I help you both? What are you up to now?"

Chicory replied, in all seriousness, "We want to find Red Tod a friend to snuffle with along the berry bushes, and we want him to meet young Vixie at the other end of the village, but how?"

Mimosa placed her tiny finger to her cheek and contemplated this request. A broad, sunny, beaming smile emerged instantaneously. "Why, I know just the way! Our beloved foxes have a wondrous sense of smell...let me tell you how to effect

a meeting and for them to think it has happened without our intervention." She whispered into Chicory's ear and that smile radiated from her face to Chicory's.

Chirrup interrupted, "Tell me, tell me, it was my idea!"

Next, as the afternoon waned into evening, Red Tod, his belly full of wondrous berries, circled three times to snooze it off. Why three times he did not know, merely that it was something he always did, just like wolves in the wild, or maybe your own pet dog. The trio of fairies, waiting until he snored gently, then circled his gleaming body and began to gently groom him with twigs and makeshift brushes. Once they had some glossy fur in their little fairy knapsacks, they took off again and made their way all along the bridleway, gently dropping a glistening, fine red hair here and there. Eventually, they got to Vixie's abode.

She was sitting quietly…feeling just a teeny bit lonely. She had been so excited at her mum's wise words of making her own way but had to confess to feeling lonely and missing the companionship of her litter-mates, chasing and tumbling, and romping with glee.

Mimosa, Chicory and Chirrup dropped the very last of the red hairs near to the pool where Vixie would drink, then took off and giggled with delight as Vixie sniffed the air, and sniffed again… then she turned around and sniffed the ground, right where Red Tod's discarded hair lay. Intrigued, she sniffed again – A friend was nearby!!!

She jumped up, her slim, agile paws trembling with excitement.

And then she ran, and ran, sniffing and running, running and sniffing until she came upon Red Tod's glade.

Well, it did not take long for Red Tod to wake up at the excited vixen's arrival. He was delighted at such a pretty and cheerful furry person who looked a lot like him. Vixie, in return, was in awe of this handsome and gentle dog-fox.

Mimosa, Chicory and Chirrup will tell you that it all worked out just fine and, if you are very quiet, gentle and patient, you can make your way along the bridleway – either very early in the morning before breakfast, or just before tea time in the darkening dusk – and you just might come across a beautiful, red, furry family of five foxes.

When Mr and Mrs Robin Refurbish Their Nest

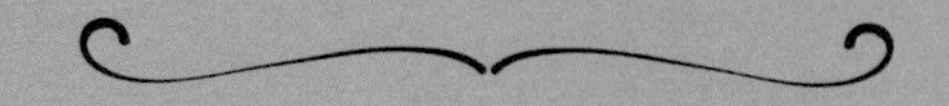

Mr Robin and his good wife Mrs Rose were in a flap. They had ventured to the garden at number 57, two doors from our fairy family. They had migrated all the way from Scandinavia and hoped to raise their family in the very garden they had arrived at. They had been greeted by Chicory and Chirrup, who delighted in regaling them with the fact that all but one of the neighbouring gardens regularly replenished their feeding stations with scrumptious fruits, seeds, suet, crushed peanuts, sunflower hearts AND raisins…a veritable feast!

What Mr Robin did not like to say to Chicory and Chirrup was the fact that, once they arrived, they had set about creating their nest. Although weary from their flight, they had pulled twigs and leaves from the bridleway which surrounded the gardens. They had found soft moss and picked and picked at it until it came away from the woody logs and he had returned time and time again to pack it into the growing nest. But still it seemed rather bare and the breeze flickered through.

He was, indeed, weary from the long flight. Their little wings had flapped and flapped all the way across the North Sea and he was so tired but felt Mrs Rose deserved the softest and most luxurious of nests.

Chirrup watched Mr Robin's little nut-brown eyes moisten and fill as he gazed upon his pretty wife. He puffed his red breast and gave a sigh, "I should so like to make our home cosy and warm for when our babies arrive."

Chirrup turned to Chicory and said, "Mr Robin needs our help and I think I know where to look."

Flapping their own gossamer-fine wings, the two kindly fairies rose above number 57 and made their way all along the bridleway until they settled at number 82. Here lived the most handsome and gentle dog, Skeet. To the fairy twins, he resembled a stunning great wolf. In truth, he was a large dog from a German Shepherd mummy and Siberian husky daddy. He was mainly black and tan in colour, but had the softest, sable undercoat (credit to his husky parentage). When his 'giants' groomed him, clumps of this undercoat remained on the brush and would float into his garden air and flutter around the ground-covering flowers and lawn.

Chirrup said, "Let's tell Skeet we need some of his soft fur for Mr and Mrs Robin's nest."

Chicory replied, "Yes, of course. That will be THE softest bedding for our friends, and when their babies arrive, they will be snug and warm, and Skeet won't need it anymore because it will keep growing back!"

As luck would have it, Skeet was dozing in his garden. Chicory fluttered down to the handsome, kind dog's ear and lifted it gently. "Hey, Skeet, how can you get your giants to brush your coat so we can have some of your unwanted fur for our feathery friends' nest?"

Skeet raised his head and chuckled at his fairy visitors. "Watch this!" he said, laughing in his deep gentle voice. With that, he raised his back leg and started scratching vigorously at his ear and neck.

Chicory and Chirrup were puzzled...why was he doing this? As if by magic, the garden door flew open and Skeet's 'giants' flew out.

"Skeet, Skeet, have you got an itch? Hope you haven't got any unwanted visitors!"

Chicory and Chirrup, hiding in the daisies behind Skeet, queried, "Do they mean us?"

Then, the giants continued, "Get Skeet's brush, he had better not have fleas. We should groom him right now."

"Fleas?" laughed the fairy twins. They knew fleas to be even tinier than them. Pesky and itchy, the fairies knew that giants always, always wanted rid of such visitors.

With that, the female giant returned with a large, square-headed silver topped brush. She brushed, and brushed. Skeet rolled playfully and smiled at the attention, he continued to smile as clumps and bunches of the fine, soft fur fluttered past him, and over in the direction of the fairies.

Chicory and Chirrup gathered these clumps and enjoyed the soft feel of each fur-ball as it wafted towards them. Soon, it was as if they were themselves in a cloud in the sky, so much fur gathered and held in their fairy arms. They blew kisses to Skeet as he continued to bask in his giants' attention. Skeet in turn

winked a gentle brown eye at them. He truly was the kindest soul and always happy to share.

Once the pair could hold no more, they rose from the daisies again and, by now, in a much slower fashion, flew not quite so high, back to number 57. Mr Robin and Rose were fiddling about, still trying to make the nest a little more appealing. The fairies braked hard and fronds of fur fell from their arms into the nest.

"It's a 'housewarming' gift for you both from gentle Skeet," they tinkled and laughed.

The Robins were delighted and nuzzled each other in unison then turned to the kindly fairies. "How can we thank you? This is so very soft and snug, and still warm! Our baby fledglings won't want to leave us. You have given us the prettiest, softest nest in the whole of the neighbourhood."

Chicory and Chirrup clapped their hands with glee. "Don't thank us, thank Skeet at number 82. If you make your way into that garden from time to time, you will be able to redecorate whenever you wish!"

And so, in the fullness of time, a clutch of five baby robins snuggled into the cosy bedding, supplied by gentle Skeet. Their parents flew in and out, bringing yummy foods to eat and, it was true, those fledglings certainly did not hurry to leave; they knew they had THE loveliest of home comforts and were as safe and cosy as they could possibly be.

Pool Party at Number 61

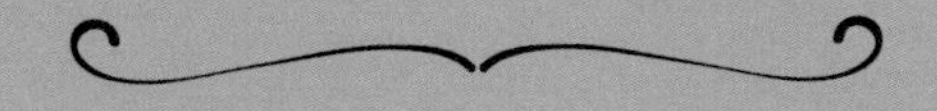

Starlight perched on the lowest branch of the magnolia tree at number 61. She had noticed the giants there huffing and puffing and carrying a large, dark brown object down the garden into a shady spot. She watched as they pushed and slid and moved this object into various places within the end of their garden. She smiled as they finally stopped and declared "This will be our pond". With that, the male giant turned back to the long snaking hosepipe and turned on the tap. A trickle was followed by a torrent of cool water into the round object. Starlight wondered what this circular object was but didn't have to wait too long.

"What a lovely cask...I am sure I can still smell the whisky," the female giant declared, laughing. Starlight watched as the cask continued to fill with sparkling water, gushing in circles around and around the barrel-like object. Next, the pair trotted to the other end of their garden and returned with bricks and boulders, dropping them at random into this cask of water. Next came greenery...large lilies, small duckweed, water hyacinth, floating heart... Starlight knew them all from the rivers around the village, and from other ponds in giants' gardens. She was intrigued as the couple finished their labours and, with that, went off for a 'cup of tea'.

Starlight fluttered from the magnolia to the edge of this new 'pond'. She dipped her teeny weeny toe into the cool water and delighted in the bubbles that were so refreshing on such a hot day. She smiled to herself and then she had the most amazing thought.

She trilled a tinkling whistle and waited for her fairy family to return. Nimbus, her beloved husband, was too far away. He toiled in farmers' fields for long hours, repairing broken crops and finding water to add to muddy pig pens for piggies to wallow in. He also cleared tracks for migrating newts to keep them safe from predatory creatures. So, today, Starlight trilled and awaited her fairy children. Sure enough, Mimosa fluttered down. Bright yellow and gleaming with delight at her mum's call. Next, those sturdy boys, Lychen and Moss, arrived...cool and muddy; they seemed not to feel the heat as the temperature around them soared. Probably because they liked to play and work in shadier spots. Chicory and Chirrup arrived last...Chirrup had to be dragged away from a flock of starlings with whom he was trying to speak to each and every one of them! And there were at least 50!

Starlight clapped her tiny hands and beamed at her children! "We are going to have a pool party. It is so very hot, and there is a beautiful, cool pool we can dip into and swim and play in."

The children exclaimed, "Where is this pool? Do you mean the small pond where giants cast fishing nets?"

"No, no, no," Starlight beamed again, "look behind this magnolia tree."

All of her children peeked past her and then squealed with

delight! “A pool party! Yes, yes, YES! We can invite Spot and Dot, our favourite ladybugs...they will love to drift across such a beautiful pool.”

“And Greengrass that busy grasshopper. He must be sooo very hot, hopping as he does across all the gardens,” Chicory added.

“And...we MUST tell all those busy worker bees that are working so hard to make honey...they need to cool down because they work so hard!” exclaimed Chirrup.

And so, whilst the giants cooled down with their cup of tea, the fairies of number 55 scattered around the gardens and bridleway, rallying all of their flying friends – damson flies, dragon flies, grasshoppers, ladybirds – or ladybugs, whatever you might care to call them – bees, butterflies and friendly birds to enjoy a pool party at number 61.

I didn’t see it myself, but I hear there were floating buttercups to lie on, berry balls to bounce on the water, honey to sup from the grateful bees, and all the fairy folk, feathery folk and flying folk had the most fun they could ever remember on such a hot and sunny day. Starlight delighted in the chattering and splashing of her fairy children and their fluttering friends. And, unbeknownst to her, the ‘giants’ gazed upon their pond and, of course, could only see the dragonflies and butterflies skimming their ‘pond’ and delighted in their enjoyment all the same. Our fairies, meanwhile, continued to be unseen...

And then Starlight had a further, exciting thought...when the winter came with its freezing air and snowy flakes, maybe, just maybe they could enjoy the giants' 'skating rink'. But that was for another day. Today was for splashing, supping, chirruping and skimming across bubbles and waves, without a care in the world. Just how Starlight liked it.

Not All Spiders Are Scary

Spinner is a spindly spider and that is a fact that nobody can dispute. When she is seen by 'big giants' and 'tiny giants', she is well-used to screams followed by giant footsteps running from her room. But Spinner has taken up residence in a tiny corner of a room where she does have company. Lucy is the gentle 'tiny giant' who it seems has been very, very poorly. Lucy stays in her bed and is tended to by her giant mum. Lucy is pale and small, and has to be propped in her bed in their bungalow home. It is a bungalow on the bridleway, as Lucy cannot make steps or stairs as she recovers from what Spinner thinks must be a very nasty illness.

Spinner quietly and secretly spins in her corner which is concealed by Lucy's bedside cabinet, on which are medicine bottles, glasses of cool water or fruity juices which the giant mum changes and replenishes frequently.

Spinner notes that Lucy weeps quietly when she is totally alone. She picks up a book or a shiny object from which she gleans pictures and music, but Spinner worries that Lucy is sad and cannot, because of her illness it seems, have visitors other than her giant parents.

Spinner was spinning diligently one day and a thought struck her. She would call upon her friends in the garden to try and cheer dear little Lucy. Spinner started to creep from her corner, but, of course, it was a sprint when all of her eight legs worked up to speed. Lucy missed this, thankfully, or she may have screamed the bungalow down. Spinner made her way to the window which was ajar, and hopped atop the window sill. From there, she could see Spot and Dot the ladybirds – or ladybugs as they are sometimes referred to. She could see Painted Lady Butterfly Betty, Billy and Bobby Bee and then her eight eyes fell upon each of the fairy children, all together on this morning, chattering and laughing as they always did.

"Hey, you all!" Spinner called. "How do you feel about making a tiny giant's day?" All turned and fluttered forward. Spinner had her audience. "My tiny giant room companion is poorly and sad. I would love to surprise her with something pretty or yummy. Any thoughts?"

The fairies and their friends pondered this awhile.

Mimosa, beaming in yellow, delighted in her reply, "Why Spinner, of course we can help…we will bring your tiny giant some gifts indeed."

With that, they busied themselves plucking scented rose petals, stringing a daisy chain, blowing dandelion heads and casting wishes for Lucy's recovery and planning further treats. Lychen and Moss flapped their wings and rose over the bridleway, over into the farmer's field and orchard. There on the ground lay the sweetest apples and pears, ripe for the plucking, so the farmer would not miss one of each. Chicory and Chirrup next hovered over the blackberry bushes and filled their knapsacks with the delicious, juiciest berries fit to burst. Then, Starlight had a brainwave! The tiny kittens at number 70, just a few doors from Lucy, were very inquisitive and of an age when they might leave their furry mummy for a new home! She fluttered up and up then moved directly to number 70. Four silver and black kittens were scampering and rolling, jumping and clutching at each other, nibbling and cackling gently with happiness. Starlight hovered a moment then dropped down to sleepy mum who was watching her kittens with a sleepy eye. Starlight whispered into Molly's ear and mum, Molly, a beautiful sleek black cat, stretched and yawned, then nodded with a smile. Starlight was merely borrowing a tiny young inquisitive kitten to come and say "hello" to the lonely Lucy.

With that, the kindly fairies and their friends flew to Lucy's windowsill where the window was ajar. Making their way in noiselessly, they dropped petals around her pillow, draped a daisy chain around her lamp and glass. Next, they propped a small, plump pear next to her glass of water. Behind that was a rosy red apple, shiny and juicy awaiting a small mouth to bite into it and enjoy. Finally, they did not need to coax Kitty. For he was up and straight onto Lucy's bed; his tail in a question mark begging the answer...will you love me and cuddle me?

Lucy awoke with a start...she had smelt the blackberries and saw a beautiful silver face gazing straight into hers. Green eyes blinking with merriment and love. She laughed and immediately cuddled the sweet and friendly kitten as the fairies gazed upon this scene.

And, in the fullness of time, the giants at number 80, although utterly baffled at the arrival of such beautiful and scented gifts, could not deny that the arrival of Kitty had well and truly sealed Lucy's recovery and, of course, she was allowed to keep and love her furry nurse and they are firm friends to this day. Spinner, meanwhile, spins without a sound, and continues her gentle observation from behind the bedside cabinet.

When Acrobatic Squirrels Navigate a Zip Wire

Most of us have seen grey squirrels, lots of people have seen red squirrels but, readers, did you know there are black squirrels in very few and far between places?

Secretive and shy, black squirrels are few in numbers, but just as agile and acrobatic as their grey and red cousins.

Jet and Peanut live along the bridleway. They are extremely agile and nimble, and navigate each tree with breath-taking swings and jumps. They giggle with delight as each out-jumps the other and then overtakes with pride and glee.

It is even more exciting when the village dogs are walked. Panting and pulling on their leads and harnesses, the local dogs are desperate to chase these two acrobats. Even off their lead, none can catch the intrepid duo, despite barking and jumping up at the foot of a tree, Jet and Peanut are gone! Gone from sight in the leafy green.

Lychen and Moss revel in their antics and can only catch up when their wings are shaken out at full capacity. Laughing, they call out to the furry-tailed twins.

Today Peanut and Jet were peckish…they had run and skipped, and flown from tree to tree. Now, after such energy bursts, their tummies were grumbling.

"Hey Moss, Lychen, can you tell us where lunch is being served?"

The fairy twins looked at each other and laughed. "Well, we did see giants at number 59 rigging up a feeding station, but we think it's intended for the local birdies."

Jet and Peanut huffed at this and replied, "But we bet they are not as hungry as us! We have flown and jumped for miles and miles."

"Where is number 59 and how do we get to the delicious food?"

Lychen and Moss fluttered their mud-coloured wings and rose upwards. "Follow us."

With that, the quartet made their way, flying, crashing through branches, rising (fairies) and somersaulting (squirrels) through the bridleway until number 59 suddenly appeared.

All four stopped at the sight of lines of giant garments; shirts, pyjamas, tea towels, underclothes fluttering in the breeze. Beyond these lines, there stood 'the feeding station' of various tables, hanging feeders and saucers. Jet and Peanut took deep breaths then, 'Lift off,' they bellowed in unison.

Lychen and Moss marvelled at their antics: rolling, swinging, tiptoeing and sliding; the duo navigated the wires as if they were tumbling on a circus 'high wire' or a zip wire across a canyon.

In no time at all, the two friendly and cheeky black squirrels were chomping and munching, at a great speed, peanuts, pieces of apple, more peanuts and other delicacies that the fairies could not make out, such was the speed that the two filled their cheek pouches for a rainy day!

"Looks like lunch is served," said Lychen. " I do hope the

birds get a look-in."

Moss shook his head. "We had better get going before we are told off by the local flocks for giving away the new takeaway."

Peanut and Jet carried on munching and, if they had only had thumbs, they would have given a resounding 'thumbs up' to the fairies for the fun of the wires and the delicious food at the end of them.

When Merlin Makes a Mistake and 'Moves'

Merlin is an inquisitive and bold cat. You might say he is 'nosy'; always popping his tiny, button nose, which is the colour of butter, incidentally, into whatever smells interesting, chasing his small toys into the tiniest corners, skidding under heavy furniture. Merlin lives at number 70 where his humans have called their home 'Catkins' and it is a very apt name for they have a number of cats and kittens. There are elderly cats such as Donald and Edgar. There is Coco, a blind cat, as well as her sister Della, who is totally deaf. Then there is Molly, a sleek black young cat, almost panther-like, that arrived just before her four silver and black kittens did. Merlin is one of the four. They are no longer kittens as such, but young and playful, 'nosy' and brave.

On this particular day, Merlin had been sauntering along the path which fronted the houses. He was suddenly aware of a strange but appealing smell, or rather a collection of smells. He did not know, of course, because he was so very young, but the smells were a combination of beeswax polish, wood varnish, fragrant washing soaps and then boxes of freshly laundered linens and towels. The family at number 62 were moving home. The man had a new job in the next county and today was the day they were leaving for a new house and home.

Merlin crinkled his nose and blinked his eyes. Such warm,

comforting smells that invited him to take a peek and so he jumped up to smell just a little bit more. He sprang like a panther into the vast, cavernous 'box' from where these smells wafted. Gingerly, he crept and hopped between boxes and piles, and still the wafts kept coming. He came upon a box of soft towels and linens and they smelt flowery and clean. He suddenly felt a little bit sleepy and decided to hop on top and curl into a ball. The smell surrounded his quivering whiskers and he smiled. Such a lovely smell. He would snooze for just five minutes and then drop down and go home.

But, as he snoozed so he suddenly awoke with a start. The big square 'room' in which he was snoozing became totally black – with a bang. He did not realise a door had been slid down and locked tight. Next, he heard a thunderous rumble and his bed started to move!

He jumped up and was, indeed, thundering along atop those soft and scented towels. For what seemed like his whole lifetime (of four months to be exact), he trundled along until there was a braking and the box whined and stopped. He heard deep voices and then a door opened.

"Did you tie down that cabinet, mate?" a deep male voice enquired. He could not hear what the reply was, but suddenly his 'room' became filled with daylight again as the door rolled upwards. With one movement, Merlin was up and flying from his soft launchpad, straight past two gawping men, both of whom were clutching a sandwich which smelt just like tuna – something

Merlin would usually absolutely love! Now, Merlin ran from the vehicle, emblazoned with 'The Moving Maestros' on its side, and straight into the farmer's field just beyond the layby.

Merlin ran and ran and did not dare look back. Where was his mum Molly and all his kitty-cat family? He suddenly felt very hungry and thirsty and did not know where he was running, so he stopped. He just wanted his mummy again and wished he hadn't been so nosy and inquisitive.

Poor Merlin did not know what to do, nor where he was. But, he was not to know that Darcy and Dill, two affectionate doves that frequented his garden, along with Mick and Maggie, a pair of magpies, had watched his adventure. Without him knowing, these four birds had soared upwards and flown alongside the vehicle emblazoned with 'The Moving Maestros'. They were prepared to follow it even if it had arrived at its destination in the next county. They were fond of Merlin and his litter-mates because all the cats at 'Catkins' had been taught to play with their toys only and not chase birds or mice into their humans' home.

As the vehicle had stopped in the layby, they were delighted to spot that Nimbus was working in the farmer's field. He was busying himself, overseeing the local newts travelling to the man-made tunnels to make their way back to the bridleway, and from there, the ponds of their birth. In fact, Merlin had not travelled very far at all, only five minutes, but to him, it felt like hundreds of miles. Nimbus was sturdy and hardworking, jolly and kind, and his sons Lychen and Moss, particularly, resembled him very much.

"Nimbus, hey Nimbus?" trilled Mick the Magpie. "Any chance your fairy family might escort this stowaway back to his garden?"

Nimbus looked across at the sad little silver and black kitten. "Have you had enough adventures for today then?"

Merlin nodded and a little silver tear trickled onto his tiny, butter-coloured nose. "I want my mummy, and I want my dinner."

With that, Nimbus pulled out his fairy horn and blew a blast. Within moments, Mimosa, Chicory and Chirrup, Lychen and Moss arrived from various gardens, branches and pathways. They smiled kindly at Merlin for it was his brother that had moved into a bungalow and become the companion of a very poorly little girl, Lucy. Indeed, that kind kitten's arrival had brought her such joy that she had recovered almost completely by now.

Now, they knew they had to get Merlin home. "Follow us," Lychen said. "We know your house and your mummy, follow us home."

And so, after only about half a mile, which to Merlin had felt like 500, the band of fairies hopped, skipped, flew a little, and smiled affectionately at Merlin, to take him all the way back to 'Catkins' at number 70.

Merlin determined there and then he would never, ever, poke his nose where it was not meant to be. His mum, Molly, nuzzled him and pushed him to the bowl of fresh tuna in a motherly attempt to cheer him up. But, in all honesty, she had not even noticed he had left, but she let him regale Donald and Edgar, Coco and Della all the same about his adventures, and his rescue

by the fairies at number 55.

Darcy and Dill, Mick and Maggie, meanwhile, sat around the bird bath, with the fairies, and chuckled. Their rescue mission was the most fun they could all remember and Merlin had been so very grateful not to have moved, by mistake, after all.

Nimbus Navigates a New Route for Newts

Nimbus is such a hard-working fairy. His fairy children at number 55 love and admire their fairy father. He is kind and gentle, yet strong and dependable. He works very hard to set an example to his fairy children and, apart from some mischievous episodes, they broadly work hard too to make nice things happen for their neighbouring creatures and 'giants'.

Nimbus works long hours in farmers' fields and orchards. He is usually found propping up broken wheatsheaves. Enlisting the help of Spinner, a friendly local spider, with spun 'ropes', he ties broken stems and ensures that the corn or wheat grows, in height, to fullness to blow in the gentle breeze. He spends many, many hours also filling acorn cups with water and travelling to and from pig pens on the farm, dropping water into puddles to ensure that the friendly pigs have wet mud to wallow in, sniffing, hoinking and rolling with pleasure.

At night, Nimbus is renowned for his gentle and efficient nurturing of migrating newts. When number 55 was built, along with all the other houses on the other side of the bridleway, the 'giants' responsible for the building works realised they had to make arrangements for the safe travel of migrating newts. Narrow tunnels were created beneath the roads, and fences erected to ensure safe onward journeys.

However, Nimbus decided quite early on that he would escort the newts and their young efts as it wasn't very often they needed to cross, and he was most keen that they travelled safely. He knew from Starlight and his children that there was a new 'pond' at number 61 and he was determined that the vulnerable travellers would make it to a safe, breeding spot.

So, on this evening, he positioned himself at the entrance to the tunnel. Sounding his horn, he was delighted that Lychen and Moss, his sturdy and dependable sons, arrived in response, in spite of the dark skies. Fluttering their wings, they whistled and called to the dark evening air.

Soon enough, the three handsome and kind fairies were conscious of the blue-green glow, not unlike Starlight's shimmering hues, as the first of the amphibians approached the tunnel. Blinking and glinting, their eyes reflected the moonlight as the moon beamed and gazed upon the scene. Gently, and efficiently, Nimbus directed the first of the procession. This was a friendly, outgoing frog, delighted to be escorted to new waters. Froggie was followed by newts, their young efts, toads and toadlets...all shimmering and glimmering in the moonlight.

"This way, follow us," called Nimbus. "It's really not so far and there is a lovely pond awaiting you."

The froglets and toadlets beamed up at their parents. "For us? How exciting!"

Some of the newts knew where they were headed already and made their way purposefully along the narrow tunnel, back

to streams and waters they knew and that beckoned them. Nimbus looked back, beaming himself at the procession. He was delighted that, once again, his mission was successful and all the glowing night-loving creatures were avoiding those huge, noisy mechanical machines on giant wheels with their blinding lights. Croaking and humming, hopping and crawling, the land and water-loving creatures made their way. Lychen and Moss kept checking that there were no stragglers; all were fit enough for their journey and did not need to be escorted. Occasionally, the two might prop up a chunkier toad or tickle the feet of a lazy newt, to encourage them to move on.

At last, after so many metres, that felt like a million miles to some, Nimbus clapped his hands and announced, "This is number 61. There is a cool, shady pool, filled with lilies and greenery to shield you. You will be safe here, those of you that are just starting out on the adventure of life."

Hundreds of yellow-glowing eyes blinked back at him in gratitude. "Thank you, as always, Nimbus, you have escorted us safely and we have all made it."

Of course, many, many newts, frogs and toads knew just where they wanted to be and did, indeed, proceed to various streams and ponds along the bridleway and beyond. But, the pond at number 61 did, I hear, become home to Froggie the froglet at the very front of the queue, and in time, tadpoles emerged into the cool waters, beneath the lilies, to start their life and this cycle all over again. Nimbus knew he would be there again, at such time he was needed, to nurture the newts to their new homes.

When TooWhit's Tower Is Tidied Up

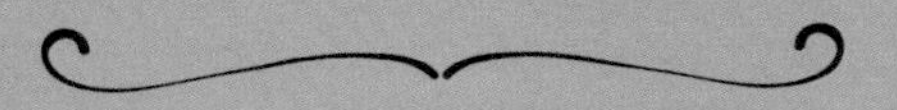

At two months old, TooWhit was an owlet who had just left home. His doting parents had hunted and fed him and his sister TooWhoo faithfully and regularly. Now TooWhit was puffed up with pride at having found his own roost upon which to perch and live.

His sister had found herself a spot in a derelict barn and had busied herself making it homely. TooWhit, much as he admired her home, felt he would rather have a spot from where he could watch other birds and creatures coming and going; if truth be told, he didn't really want to be alone and away from the comings and goings of the other creatures in the gardens and bridleway. Of course, in the fullness of time, if he had a partner and his own owlets, a barn might be just fine but that was for the future.

And so, for now, TooWhit had found a strong, tall tree with a natural 'V' fork upon which he could perch quite comfortably. 'Quite' was the word, however. He had to admit that there were a few spiky pieces of bark that snagged his bottom as he settled into the 'V'. It was such a wonderful spot, and he was suitably elevated to not be visible during his sleeping daylight hours and, so remain safe, that he wished and wished to find a way to make it just that teeny bit more comfortable.

He sat very early one morning, his broad facial features and huge unblinking eyes, not unlike a cat's, were focussing on a small band of fairies. We readers know it was our fairy family at number 55, because this tree was directly on the bridleway, behind the garden at number 55, where the track led to the neighbouring village. TooWhit was mesmerised as he watched them laughing and tinkling as they concentrated on a project before them. His expert vision picked out Mimosa, Chicory and Chirrup, and their mum Starlight. He puzzled to watch them weaving and stitching petals and small feathers into soft, small squares. Spinner, a spindly spider sprinted to them from time to time with fine lines of thread which they busily and gratefully received, and wove into these small patchworks.

Finally, TooWhit could watch no longer without asking. "WooHoo, WooHoo," he called.

Immediately, the shiny, smiley faces turned upward to the V-shaped fork in the tree.

Still laughing and tinkling, Mimosa called up, "Hey, how come you are awake? We thought you should be asleep during the daytime and awake at night?"

TooWhit still did not blink as he replied, "I would be asleep but I am really curious as to what you are doing and making? You are so very busy and I am fighting sleep to see the finished outcome."

It was Chirrup who next looked up, beaming and smiling kindly. "We are making a cushion for YOU to perch on. We have watched you wriggling and squirming with sharp pieces of bark poking

into your feathers. We understand that is a perfect vantage point for you, and we wanted to make it more comfortable for you."

Chicory added, "We have collected discarded feathers from several gardens, some soft petals and hay, we have also woven plump daisies into several chains. Then we called into a gentle dog Skeet's garden for some of his soft, brushed fur. And, finally, clever spider Spinner has kindly made and donated the thread to thread them all together into a padded cushion. So, we are sorry it is no longer a surprise, but we will pop up shortly and make it fit."

And, with that, Mum Starlight shook out her shimmering wings in duck-egg blue. She received the padded cushion from her three fairy children and rose upwards. TooWhit did, at last, blink. And he blinked with pleasure as Starlight busied herself, smiling all the time, as she gently prodded his posterior until he lifted a little. Then she slid the softest, plumpest cushion into the jagged, snaggy V of the tree. TooWhit plopped back down again and could no longer feel the sharp shards on the old sturdy tree.

"Thank yoooooo," he said, his big eyes moistening and glistening as, truthfully, he felt he could weep at the fairy family's kindness, and that of Spinner and Skeet further along the gardens.

"I am so going to love living here, and having you all as neighbours. You have been the kindest and most generous of neighbours and I thank you."

And it is true, TooWhit had absolutely no reason to move away from his perfect perch, and if you are out very, very early in the morning, you just might see him nestling and snuggling down for a good day's sleep.

SOS for Cindy the Cygnet in a Spin

Chicory and Chirrup were concentrating but still smiling and tinkling with laughter and chatter. They were perched upon small mounds, hidden within bullrushes and reeds at the water's edge. The lake where they sat was in the village, a mere 10-minute walk for giants from the bridleway, or indeed from their own home and garden at number 55. Several giants whiled away many hours at this lake, casting out their rods to catch fish. Chicory and Chirrup watched them often, and smiled as these giants jumped from boxes or seats at the beep of an alarm, as a careless carp or bream fish mistook the giant's 'bait' for a tasty morsel. Chicory and Chirrup were mightily relieved that, once the careless carp or dozy bream had landed upon the bank, so the giant studied his 'catch', maybe weighed it, then carefully and gently returned it to the lapping edges of the bankside.

Today, Chicory and Chirrup were amusing themselves painting stones with tiny fairy images of flower petals, butterflies or pretty feathers. The paint they used came from berries and over-ripe fruits they had pushed through their mum Starlight's tiny, fairy sieve. Then they added splashes of water and their paint was ready. The twins often painted little stones and then delighted in popping them on various stages of the track, under bobbing flower heads, away from the stinging nettles, in order that tiny giants might come upon them and marvel at the pretty pictures that looked so natural, and wonder just where they had come from.

Today, as they tinkled, painted and chattered, so they were interrupted by a sudden sharp breeze as the sun gave way to a dark shadow. Corky the Cormorant had descended from his mighty roost, where he surveyed the lake, always looking out for his next feed. He swooped directly to the chattering pair. He was black and sleek, serious and not usually very good-humoured if truth be told.

They looked up. Chirrup always liked to talk to all birds, large imposing birds like Corky, or tiny and chatty like little Wendy Wren. “Hey, Corky, where has the sun gone? You are so mighty, you have created the largest of shadows.”

Corky puffed with pride, then responded, “I have just seen something that I do not like the look of and wonder if you might help?”

Intrigued, Chicory and Chirrup popped down their tiny paint brushes and looked into Corky’s beady eyes that glinted from tufty feathers.

When Corky realised he had their attention, he continued, “Cobb and Penny, you know our resident swans, have five cygnets. I have been watching Cindy, the smallest cygnet, struggling at the edge of the lilies. I think she has caught her foot in some wire from a giant’s fishing rod. She is splashing and worrying, and it won’t come off. Can you help?”

"Oh dear," replied Chicory. Her little fairy face had suddenly stopped smiling and was very, very serious. "We must go to Cindy straightaway."

The two fairies flapped their violet-hued gossamer wings and rose from the secret reedy spot. Up and up they flew, looking down upon the dragon and damsel flies skimming the lake. Ducks and geese cruised the waters, honking and quacking, seemingly oblivious to the cygnet's alarming situation.

They came upon a splashing and honking as poor Cindy desperately tried to unravel the wire. She was circling and flapping; her family had been drifting gently some yards away, but had now returned to their baby and the mum was flapping and squawking in helplessness.

Chirrup, although a cheeky and cheerful fairy, was also devoted to all birds, in both the gardens and around the waters. He turned to Chicory and said, "I am going in!"

With that, he dived into the cool, green waters and made his way deftly to poor Cindy's foot. There, sure enough, was a length of fine fishing wire. It was caught tight around her webbed foot. Chirrup tried to tug it away but it was bound fast. He had to think quickly. As he was thinking, so he became aware that his twin, Chicory had joined him. Under the water, she swiftly made her way to the bound wire. Standing above it, she hovered briefly then forced her tiny fairy body between the wire and Cindy's foot. Up and down she bounced and, with each movement, the wire dislodged a teeny bit more. Chirrup, meanwhile, found the end of the wire and taking it in his tiny fairy hand, pulled it and then swam round and round, unravelling the loosening bind. As he swam, poor Chirrup became giddier and giddier at the rotations. At last, after what seemed like hours of effort, the wire became slack and Cindy gently kicked her webbed foot to release it. The fairy twins gathered up the wire and rose through the cool green waters. Once at the surface, Penny the mother swan flapped her huge wings in delight.

"Chirrup, Chicory, you are the bravest, kindest fairies on this lake. How can we ever thank you?"

Chicory and Chirrup turned to each other and then back to Penny. "It is enough for us to see that Cindy is safe and no longer frightened. Please remind her to keep away from the giants when they are fishing."

Cindy looked down and nodded that she certainly would! She would admit to her devoted mum later that she was intrigued at the scent of the giant's bait and just wanted to get a little closer.

And so, after their heroics, the modest fairy twins returned to their secret spot and painted some more pretty stones. Glancing up at the willow tree, they smiled at Corky, and he winked back his beady eye, beneath the tufty feathers, then gazed upon the lake no longer noisy with splashing, but tranquil and calm, just as they all liked it.

When Robbie and Roly's Ramble Goes Wrong!

The fairies at number 55 really like young Robbie. At seven years of age, he is cheerful, cheeky and outgoing. And he is clumsy. The fairies remember quite recently they had to round up Robbie's two rabbits Hunny and Bonnie as he had not secured their hutch door. The two cheeky bunnies had hot-hopped it from their garden at number 68 into the bridleway to meet and chatter with their 'wild' brown bunny cousins. Mimosa, Chicory and Chirrup, Lychen and Moss had to interrupt the hopping, playing and chattering, and usher the two hopaways back to the small hole in the fence, and back into their garden where Robbie's giants were able to tempt them back to their hutch with fresh orchard hay and some fresh vegetables which the two bunnies had not managed to find for themselves on their brief adventure into the wild.

Another reason the fairies like Robbie is that he can see them. Not many giants, large or tiny, can, but Robbie, for all his cheerful cheekiness, is a sensitive child too and has seen our fairies from number 55. Of course, when he told his own giant parents, they scoffed and said he had dreamt them. Fairies don't exist except in a vivid imagination.

Today, Robbie had been allowed to take his new puppy and best friend Roly for a walk along the bridleway. Roly is a roly-poly golden retriever and, at only three months, has barely started walking with his giants, but he is loving the companionship of Robbie who nagged and nagged his giants for a pet dog. Robbie still loves his bunnies, of course, but yearned for a dog to walk and play with. Robbie's giants insisted on knowing where Robbie planned to walk his pet, and were satisfied he won't go too far.

Now, this morning, the two had left the garden gate and Robbie thought he had secured the latch but, of course, in typical, clumsy Robbie fashion, it had not clicked to. The gate had closed, but the lock was undone...

Robbie and Roly were bounding along the bridleway. Roly was prancing like a young pony and gazing up at Robbie who laughed and beamed down upon his young, golden friend. For some little way, they ran a little, then walked a little. Robbie stopped every now and then to give his adoring Roly a small treat to keep his attention. However, Robbie had not noticed that, in his haste to get out and running with his pal, he had not tied his laces on his left trainer. Suddenly, as they gathered speed, the loose lace became entwined on a small twig jutting from the hedgerow. Robbie was snagged to a sharp halt and turned his left ankle.

"Oooooow!" Robbie squealed and fell with a thud on to the damp, dewy track. His ankle had twisted and the pain took his breath away. He dropped Roly's lead and the pup stopped with a start too and gazed upon his pal.

In all honesty, Robbie wanted to cry and tried and tried to stand again on the twisted ankle.

"Noooooo!" he yelped and sat back down again. Hot tears

coursed down his rosy cheeks, flushed with the running, and now the pain.

Roly gazed upon him and was not sure if this was a new game. He felt that it probably wasn't as his human wasn't including him in the fierce rubbing of the ankle.

As this little scene was taking place, Mick and Maggie, two of the local magpies, were swooping across the bridleway to number 59 where a feast of niger seeds and other delicacies awaited them on a feeding station. They took one look at the pained child, and the roly-poly pup, and flew beyond number 59, onwards to number 55.

"Hey, Mimosa!" they tweeted. "Come quickly, a small giant is in pain on the bridleway and there is a small pup who doesn't know what to do!"

Mimosa, gleaming yellow, beamed back at the handsome pair of birds.

"Oh goodness, yes of course, we will come right now." With that, she trilled for Chicory and Chirrup, Lychen and Moss to join her. They fluttered their gossamer-wings, and rose above the wall at number 55. Before long, they came upon poor Robbie and Roly. Poor Roly was not enjoying this game at all and he felt for his poor human who could not stand just yet.

Robbie looked up as he felt the breeze of the descending fairies. "Oh wow! Have you come to help me?" His eyes were like saucers as he gazed upon the five fairies who, in turn, were hovering and taking in the whole scene.

“Yes, we have come to help you. We must take Roly home for you and you must sit and wait for your giants.”

“Oh thank you, all; I really cannot stand. I have twisted my ankle!” Robbie really wanted to cry but felt he must not look like a baby in front of this cheerful band.

Mimosa touched his hot cheek and whispered to him, “Cry if you want to, we know how painful your poor ankle is. You have been very brave in front of Roly, but you must cry if it hurts.”

So Robbie did sniff a little and handed the lead to the five fairies. With that, they each held a small part of the lead because, for them, Roly was very, very heavy even though he was only a puppy.

They made their way back along the bridleway. Roly was very puzzled that it took five of these tiny, tiny folk to walk him back. But he trotted along trustingly as he sensed they were being kind and helpful. As they arrived at Robbie’s back gate, Lychen fluttered upwards. He laughed back at the others. “Typical Robbie, he has been clumsy again, but it has done us a favour as he has not locked the gate! Goodness knows how long that would have taken us to lever that latch back.” He then, with the help of Chirrup and Moss, put his fairy shoulder against the gate and the three boy fairies pushed and pushed until the gate sprung back.

They all kissed Roly’s soft, golden head and whispered to him to run back into the garden so he would be seen by Robbie’s giants. Roly did not have to be asked twice. He knew this was his garden and in he ran, yapping and barking. True enough, within moments, the giants ran into the garden at Roly's return.

"Where is Robbie?"

"How did Roly get back here? Goodness, he must be so clever to find his way home!"

With that, the startled giants flew through the gate and, as they had insisted Robbie tell them his route, they ran along the bridleway. Before long, they came upon the sitting, sobbing seven-year-old.

"Hey Robbie sweetheart, we are here, whatever happened?"

Poor Robbie was so very relieved to see his parents. Roly had, of course, gained another walk and was panting with delight at the return to his pal. The giants gently helped their son up – and mum bent down and tied his shoelace – before supporting their limping son all the way home. They regaled Robbie with the story of Roly raising the alarm and making his way home. Robbie tried to interrupt and tell them of the fairies coming to the rescue. And, do you know what? They scoffed and replied that he must have fallen asleep whilst he waited for them, and dreamt of those fairies at number 55!

The End